ODDS BODKIN

The Christmas Cobwebs

Illustrated by TERRY WIDENER

GULLIVER BOOKS • HARCOURT, INC.

San Diego   New York   London

www.harcourt.com

Gulliver Books is a trademark of Harcourt, Inc.,
registered in the United States of America and/or other jurisdictions.

Library of Congress Cataloging-in-Publication Data
Bodkin, Odds.
The Christmas cobwebs/by Odds Bodkin; illustrated by Terry Widener.
p. cm.
"Gulliver Books."
Summary: Having reluctantly parted with their treasured Christmas ornaments,
members of a German immigrant family awake on Christmas morning
to find miraculous replacements spun by spiders.
[1. Christmas—Fiction. 2. Spiders—Fiction. 3. German Americans—Fiction.]
I. Widener, Terry, ill. II. Title
PZ7.B6355Ch 2001
[E]—dc21   97-25626
ISBN 0-15-201459-4

First edition
A C E G H F D B

Printed in Singapore

The illustrations in this book were done in Golden acrylics on Strathmore Bristol board.
The text type was set in Throhand Ink.
The display type was set in Powhatten with OptiMorgan-FiveNine.
Color separations by Bright Arts Ltd., Hong Kong
Printed and bound by Tien Wah Press, Singapore
This book was printed on totally chlorine-free Nymolla Matte Art paper.
Production supervision by Sandra Grebenar and Ginger Boyer
Designed by Linda Lockowitz

In memory of my father, who told me stories

—O. B.

For my dad

—T. W.

IN OLD CHICAGO there once lived a humble cobbler. All day long the door to his shop swung to and fro as customers came and went with pairs of shoes. To stay warm he worked by his smoky coal stove, rap-tapping leather with his fine shoemaker's tools.

As Christmas drew near, he called his children to his side to tell them the story of how, before any of them had been born, he and their mother had sailed to America from Germany, deep inside a steamship.

"And do you remember what it is, the one thing we brought with us to remind us of our old home?" he asked.

"Oh yes, Papa! Yes!" the children squealed. "You brought the Box!"

"Yes, the Box," he answered, his eyes twinkling.

He climbed the stairs and in a few moments returned with a carved oak box.

The drawers of the box were lined with soft green felt, and inside them lay blown-glass ornaments. One by one the cobbler lifted them out: A golden sleigh once owned by his great-grandpapa. A silvery angel his wife had won as a girl. A star the couple had cherished since their wedding day. And many others.

"These ornaments came with us across the sea," the cobbler whispered as his wife watched, smiling. "So, children, be oh-so-careful with them. Do not break a single one. They remind us of home.

"Next week, we find a Christmas tree," promised the cobbler. "Now, off to bed."

That night as the family slept upstairs, the coal stove puffed smoke. Inside the stovepipe a soft crinkling grew louder and louder, until it became a fiery roar. Soon the stovepipe glowed red-hot. The wallpaper near it began to smoke, then burst into flame.

Upstairs the cobbler awakened. "I smell smoke! Wake up! Wake up!" he cried to his wife. "Get the children! There's a fire!"

As the family dashed downstairs, flames growled up the curtains and licked the rafters.

"The Box!" cried the cobbler, stopping. "I'll get it. Hurry! Raise the
alarm!"

He ran back through the flames. Finding the box in a corner of his
workshop, he rescued the precious ornaments.

Although firefighters soon arrived, and though they fought the fire for hours, they could not save the cobbler's shop. By dawn everything had burned to ashes. The cobbler stood in the snow, hugging his wife and children.

"But we are alive, with nobody hurt," he said, hiding his sorrow. "And look, I have the Box. Let us go."

Kind neighbors gave them food and warm clothes in a ragbag. Someone said that, twenty blocks away, at the city's edge, an old abandoned farmer's shack still stood. Clutching the oak box, the cobbler trudged off through the snow with his family.

Dust covered everything inside the little shack, and cobwebs filled the rafters. An old broom stood in a bare corner by a rusty stove. The cobbler's wife took the broom and began to clean the room. She was just about to sweep the cobwebs away when her husband touched her arm.

"Please don't take their homes," the cobbler said.

"Whose homes?" asked his wife.

"The little spiders who live up there," he answered. "We lost everything. Those webs are their homes. Let them stay."

Against her better judgment, the cobbler's wife put down her broom. Although the family heard nothing, up in the rafters, tiny legs scurried this way and that. Tiny eyes gazed down.

After the children fell asleep, the cobbler and his wife talked quietly. "Husband," she said, "what will we do?"

"In order to work, I must have new tools," he answered. "And new leather."

"But we have nothing." She began to weep.

The cobbler held his wife's hand. "That's not so, my love," he said. "We have the Box. The ornaments are worth a great deal."

"We can't sell our ornaments!" she gasped.

"But we must. We have the children to care for." He looked over at the oak box. "Don't tell them. Not yet."

The next day the cobbler went into town. For a handful of money, enough to buy tools and shoe leather, he sold the family's precious ornaments.

When Christmas Eve came, the cobbler and his children cut a little green fir tree they had found at the edge of the woods. They dragged the tree home and stood it up in their bare shack.

"It's so different here," said one child, looking around the room.

"But our ornaments will remind us of home!" said another. "Where are they, Papa?"

The cobbler lifted the children onto his lap. "Well, children," he said, holding them close, "we don't have the ornaments any longer." The children looked very surprised. "But," he went on, "we have something much more precious."

"What is that, Papa?"

"We have each other," he answered. "And look, see how beautiful our tree is? Green, with a little bit of melting snow on the branches. See how the candlelight sparkles in the drops? Those are our ornaments. So beautiful."

Although he tried to make his children happy, the cobbler felt his own heart breaking.

That night as the family slept, the house grew quiet. Then up in the rafters, tiny legs began to scurry this way and that.

At the end of a silver thread, a tiny spider dropped down toward the bare tree.

Another spider followed.

And then another and another.

On Christmas Day, the cobbler awakened. He whispered to his wife. Together they carried their children, blinking, to the tree.

"Merry Christmas, my little ones," the cobbler whispered, looking up at the rafters. "I think these ornaments are for you." The children's eyes grew wide. "Yes, go ahead, feel."

The children touched the miraculous ornaments.

"But be oh-so-careful," the cobbler added softly.

"Do not break a single one," his wife said, smiling.

"That's right." The cobbler smiled, too, hugging his loved ones close. "These ornaments remind us of home."

"Which home, Papa?" asked the children.

The cobbler gazed at their shimmering tree.
"This one, children."